Contents

Chapter One

Alby was an Alien. Sometimes he looked like this . . .

But usually, he looked like this.

I AM READING

Alien Alby

KAYE UMANSKY

ILLUSTRATED BY

SOPHIE ROHRBACH

KINGFISHER
NEW YORK

For Mo and Ella

 KINGFISHER
LONDON & NEW YORK

Text copyright © Kaye Umansky 2009
Illustrations copyright © Sophie Rohrbach 2009

Published in the United States by Kingfisher,
175 Fifth Ave., New York, NY 10010
Kingfisher is an imprint of Macmillan Children's Books, London.
All rights reserved.

Distributed in the U.S. by Macmillan, 175 Fifth Ave., New York, NY 10010
Distributed in Canada by H.B. Fenn and Company Ltd., 34 Nixon Road,
Bolton, Ontario L7E 1W2

Library of Congress Cataloging-in-Publication data has been applied for.

ISBN: 978-0-7534-3005-7

Kingfisher books are available for special promotions and premiums. For details contact:
Special Markets Department, Macmillan, 175 Fifth Avenue, New York, NY 10010.

For more information, please visit www.kingfisherpublications.com

First American Edition June 2010
Printed in China
10 9 8 7 6 5 4 3 2 1

Alby lived on an Alien planet.

He had a mom, a dad, and a sister named Arlene. Here they are, smiling. Well, Arlene isn't.

Alby had a loyal Squeeble named Squee. Squeebles are popular Alien pets. They are orange and happy. They bounce and knock things over.

Sometimes Squee looked like this . . .

And sometimes like this.

Home was a Dome. It looked like this
on the outside . . .

And this on the inside.

The Dome was very neat. Alby's mom
liked things to be just so.

The backyard was neat, too. Well, the parts you could see. There was a weedy, swampy part, but that was hidden behind the bushes.

Alby and Squee weren't allowed to play there.

Keep out! That means YOU, Alby! mum

They did, though.

Chapter Two

Alby's bedroom wasn't neat. It was
bursting with noisy Alien toys. Most
of them went *BOING!, BANG!, POP!,*
and *WHEEEE!*

He had a Groobleblaster

and a Splattermerang.

He had a Swizzelwizzel,

a Nargian Nose Flute,

and a Zoomeroo.

He ate tons of Alien cereal and sent away for free stuff. He had hundreds of Alien Animal stickers that he never got around to sticking. He had a huge collection of Space Warriors, mostly in pieces because Squee liked to chew on them.

He saved up and ordered a Wombian Wobble Board from a catalog.

He hurt himself on that one.

Alby had quiet things, too, which he kept for nighttime: his books and his toy catalogs and his old stuffed toys. His favorite was the purple thing with three heads, named Purpy.

Alby slept with Purpy. And with Squee,
of course. He always slept with Squee.

Alby had a favorite book called *Planet of the Earthlings*. It was all about funny-looking creatures who liked food called "Chips." They had pets called "Dogs," and they slept with things called "Teddy Bears."

Alby's mom wasn't happy with Alby's
toy collection. She called it a pile of old
junk. Sometimes she threw things away,
which made Alby cry all night.

Most of Alby's games required a lot of running around, so his mom made him play outside.

He played with the Zoomeroo until it broke.

He squirted Squee with the Splattermerang.

He Groobleblasted
Squee, too! That
was fun! Then
they ran around
again.

Somehow, they ended up in the muddy
part of the backyard where they weren't
allowed. And that's how the trouble
started.

Chapter Three

"What's this on the carpet?" asked Alby's
mom. "It's mud, isn't it?"

"Is it?" said Alby.

"Yes. And you know how it got there,
don't you?"

"Do I?"

"Yes. You brought it in. You and Squee."

"I wiped my feet," said Alby.

"Squee didn't, though, did he? You're supposed to remind him. He's your responsibility. You were down in the swamp again, weren't you? What did I say about that?"

"We just sort of fell there by accident."

"Well, you can get those spots out and then go to your room. And take Squee with you."

It took forever to clean the carpet.
Alby's mom nagged, and Squee sat in
a corner, looking small
and sad.

Then Alby went to his room.

"This is all your fault," he grumbled.

"I keep telling you to wipe your feet."

He did. But Squee always forgot. He

was a Squeeble. They are good at

playing and squealing, but they have

terrible memories.

Chapter Four

It wouldn't have been so bad if it hadn't

happened again the next day. They

shouldn't have gone to the swampy part,

of course, but it had been raining during the night. Alien rain makes great mud for sliding.

This time, cleaning the carpet took
even longer. Squee was put outside
in disgrace.

He was still there at dinnertime.

For dinner, they had Woodlydoodlynoodly
Strings. They ate them using fiddle sticks,
which are like revolving prongs.

But Alby wasn't hungry.

"Can't he come in now?" he asked.

"Eat your Strings," said his mom. "You, too, Arlene."

"I don't like Woodlydoodlynoodly Strings," said Arlene. "I want food that sounds shorter."

"Like 'chips,'" said Alby. "That's what they eat in *Planet of the Earthlings*."

"You'll eat what you're given," said his mom. "Ah, here's your dad."

In came Alby's dad with something in his arms.

"Okay," he said, setting it on the table.

"This should do the trick."

Oh! Oh, *no!*

It was a Squeeble Dome!

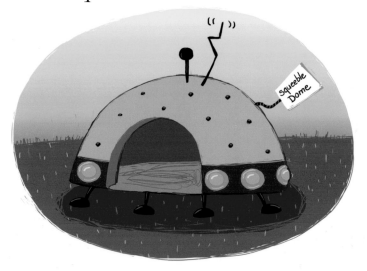

"I hope that's not for Squee," said Alby.

But it was. Even Arlene was shocked.

"We warned you enough times," said

Alby's mom.

"But he always sleeps with me!"

"Not anymore," said his dad. "He has

his own Dome now. He'll love it."

Chapter Five

But Squee didn't love his Dome. He hated it. It was small and drafty. But worst of all, it was far away from Alby. "You'll be all right," said Alby. "I'll bring you some dinner."

Squee licked Alby's elbow and said,

"Squee." But there wasn't any joy in it.

And he didn't want any dinner.

"I know," said Alby. "I'll bring out the

Splattermerang. You like that, don't you?"

But Squee wasn't interested in the Splattermerang. Or the Swizzelwizzel. He didn't even cheer up when Alby played him a tune on the Nargian Nose Flute.

"Stop making that racket and come inside!" shouted Alby's mom. "It's bedtime!"

"You'll be all right," Alby said again to Squee. "I have to go now."

And he gathered up all the unwanted
toys and went inside to bed.

He didn't sleep, though. He lay hugging
Purpy, thinking about poor little Squee
outside, all on his own in the night, with
nothing to comfort him. Whatever could
he do?

Squee shivered in his Dome. It was raining again. He wished that he was in Alby's room, on Alby's bed. Why was he here? He didn't know. He was only a Squeeble.

His fur pricked up when he heard a footstep. Then he smelled a familiar smell.

"Here," whispered Alby. "Have him.
See you in the morning."
It was Purpy. Purpy smelled like Alby.
It wasn't perfect, but it was the next best
thing. Both of them slept well in the end.

Chapter Six

The next morning, Alby and Squee were
on their very best behavior. Squee didn't
break anything, and neither of them
went near any mud. In the afternoon
they sat in the backyard reading *Planet
of the Earthlings*.

Later, Alby looked at a new catalog that had just arrived. There was something really good in it. Something very expensive, but great!

That night, Squee slept in his Dome again, but he had Purpy, so it wasn't too bad.

Alby lay in bed, planning.

The following day, Alby's mom let him hold a Grand Toy Sale outside the gate.

He sold the
Groobleblaster,

the Splattermerang, and the Wombian

Wobble Board.

He sold the

Swizzelwizzel

and the Nargian

Nose Flute.

He gave away the

broken Zoomeroo. He got

rid of the chewed-up Space Warriors.

Nobody wanted the stickers, so he was stuck with them. He sold everything else except Purpy.

There still wasn't quite enough money, but Arlene chipped in, which was nice of her. Then Alby sent away for . . .

. . . a *Luxury Squeeble Feet Cleaner!*
It was fully automated, with little
revolving brushes. Here it is, right by
the back door:

Squee loved the Feet Cleaner, because
it tickled. He never forgot to use it.

In the end, he was allowed back indoors to sleep with Alby—and with Purpy, of course.

They didn't need the Squeeble Dome anymore, so Alby's mom made his dad throw it behind the bushes in the swampy part of the backyard, where Alby and Squee weren't allowed to go.

They sometimes did, though!

About the author and illustrator

Kaye Umansky was born in Devon, England, and went to London to be a teacher. She has been writing children's books for 21 years. She has a husband, a grown-up daughter, 13 fish in a tank, and two cats. She likes to read funny books. "I wish I had a Squeeble for a pet," says Kaye, "but I don't think my cats would like it."

Sophie Rohrbach was born in Strasbourg, France. She studied illustration in Lyon, where she now lives with her darling, her daughter, and her paintbrushes. Sophie is passionate about the colors and patterns that she uses in her illustrations. She loves to include details in her pictures to achieve small worlds full of fantasy and color.

Strategies for Independent Readers

Predict

Think about the cover, illustrations, and the title
of the book. What do you think this book will be about?
While you are reading think about what may
happen next and why.

Monitor

As you read ask yourself if what you're reading makes sense.
If it doesn't, reread, look at the illustrations, or read ahead.

Question

Ask yourself questions about important ideas
in the story such as what the characters might
do or what you might learn.

Phonics

If there is a word that you do not know, look carefully
at the letters, sounds, and word parts that you do know.
Blend the sounds to read the word. Ask yourself if this is
a word you know. Does it make sense in the sentence?

Summarize

Think about the characters, the setting where the
story takes place, and the problem the characters faced
in the story. Tell the important ideas in the beginning,
middle, and end of the story.

Evaluate

Ask yourself questions like: Did you like the story?
Why or why not? How did the author make the story
come alive? How did the author make the story fun to
read? How well did you understand the story? Maybe
you can understand it better if you read it again!